# JESS & JAYLEN

# MUSEUM MYSTERY

BY BLAKE HOENA • ILLUSTRATED BY DANA REGAN

Published by The Child's World®
1980 Lookout Drive • Mankato, MN 56003-1705
800-599-READ • www.childsworld.com

Acknowledgments
The Child's World®: Mary Berendes, Publishing Director
The Design Lab: Design
Red Line Editorial: Editorial direction and production

ISBN 9781631434396
LCCN 2014930634

Printed in the United States of America
Mankato, MN
July, 2014
PA02215

# TABLE OF CONTENTS

# FIELD TRIP

"I can't wait!" Jaylen said.

He had been saying that ever since he and Jess found out they were going to the Natural History Museum for their spring field trip. Now they were sitting side by side on a school bus headed for the museum.

"They have a huge display of dino teeth," Jaylen continued. "It's the coolest."

Jess rolled her eyes. They had been best friends forever, and she knew how Jaylen got. When he was excited about something, he couldn't let it go. Whether it was a new video game or dinosaur bones. He would just go on and on and on.

"This is going to be the best school trip ever," Jaylen added.

*I doubt it,* Jess thought.

She wasn't into dinosaurs. Plus, her mom was sitting in front of her. She had volunteered to be a chaperone for this field trip. Jess wasn't sure she liked having her mom along. She would have to be on her best behavior. But at least she didn't have to sit through all her classes today. So it shouldn't be too bad of a day, especially with the surprise she had for Jaylen.

Jess poked Jaylen in the arm.

"Hey, what was that for?" he asked, sounding annoyed.

"Guess what?" Jess said. "I brought a camera!"

His eyes lit up as she pulled a small camera out of her backpack.

"There'll be so many cool things to take photos of!" Jaylen said. "Did your mom buy you that?"

Jess could tell her friend was jealous. He had a cell phone, but it didn't have a camera.

"Nah, it's my sister's," she said.

"Really?" Jaylen asked, surprised. "She's letting you use it?"

"Yeah, Becky's pretty cool," Jess said.

Last year, Jess's dad had remarried. Not only did she get a new stepmom but now she also had a stepsister and a stepbrother.

"Why did she give you her camera?" Jaylen asked.

"Well, when I said we were going to the Natural History Museum," Jess said, "she offered to let me use it for the day."

"No way!" Jaylen said.

Jess tucked the camera into her backpack at her feet. She also had her lunch in the bag, along with some snacks her mom had packed.

"Actually, Becky is hoping she can get extra credit on a report by using the pictures I take," Jess said. "So I said I'd help her."

Normally Jaylen would have said something about Jess helping her sister get extra credit. It seemed a little like cheating. And he couldn't stand it when people cheated. But he also knew Jess had always hated being an only child. She didn't have any siblings to play with or hang out with. That had all changed when her dad remarried. Jaylen knew Jess would do just about anything to get her new big sister to like her. Plus, he thought it was pretty cool that they'd have a camera to use for their field trip.

# CHAPTER TWO

# MISSING!

A few minutes later, their bus bounced over a speed bump in front of the museum and then screeched to a stop. Everyone's backpacks toppled forward. Kids scrambled to gather their things.

Mrs. Johnson, Jess and Jaylen's teacher, stood up. She had been sitting in the front of the bus with Jess's mom.

"OK, everyone," Mrs. Johnson said. "Be sure to grab your bags before exiting the bus."

Jess and Jaylen picked up their backpacks. Then they crowded toward the front of the bus with their classmates.

"Hi, honey," Jess's mom said as they stepped off the bus. Jess rolled her eyes. She was always embarrassed when her mom called her "honey."

"Hey," was all Jess said as she walked past.

"Hello, Mrs. Reynolds," Jaylen said.

"Hi, Jaylen," Jess's mom said.

Once off the bus, Mrs. Johnson guided everyone to the museum's student lounge. There, they each hung their backpacks on a hook. The lounge also had chairs and tables. The class would eat lunch there later.

"While we are touring the museum, this room will be kept locked. Mrs. Reynolds will have a key to the room," Mrs. Johnson explained. "If you need to get anything from your backpacks, please ask her. Otherwise, you can wait until lunch when we gather back here to eat."

Everyone left the room. They headed toward the front desk. Their tour guide was waiting for them. He was tall, skinny, and wearing glasses.

"OK, class," he began. "Just a few quick rules before we get started. DO NOT touch or climb on any of the exhibits. They are old. Millions of years old. And they break easily. You can take pictures if you want, but please no flashes. That's it."

He waved all the students forward, toward the first exhibit.

"We're going to start our tour in the Triassic Period, when dinosaurs first stomped around," he said. "Then we'll work our way through the Jurassic Period and to the end of the Cretaceous Period, when the age of dinosaurs ended."

"Isn't this cool?" Jaylen asked Jess.

"Not really," she replied. "I don't understand half of what he's saying."

"Well, the Triassic Period—" Jaylen began.

"Booo-ring," Jess interrupted with a yawn.

"Here is a model of an Eoraptor leg bone from about 220 million years ago," the guide said, pointing to a glass case.

"You should get a picture of this," Jaylen said. "It's one of the earliest dinosaurs."

"Oh, yeah," Jess said.

She reached into her front pockets. She looked confused. Then she dug into her back pockets.

"Nuts! I forgot Becky's camera in my backpack," Jess told Jaylen. "What should I do?"

"You can get it at lunch," Jaylen said.

"But I'll miss out on all this early stuff," Jess said, looking panicked. "And then I can't help Becky with her extra credit."

"So, check with your mom," Jaylen said.

Jess scrunched up her nose. She really didn't want to talk to her mom, especially in front of her classmates. But she needed the camera. Jess had no other choice.

"Yes, honey?" her mom asked when Jess came up to her.

"I forgot something back in the student lounge," Jess said.

"Can it wait until lunch?" her mom asked, scrunching up her nose, too.

"No, it's really, really important, Mom," Jess said. "Can we go get it, please?"

"OK, OK," her mom said. "We can catch up with the group at the Camptosaurus exhibit."

Jess and her mom headed back to the student lounge. Jess's mom unlocked the door. Jess ran over to her backpack. She unzipped the main pocket. She dug around inside her bag. No camera. She unzipped all the side pockets. Still no camera.

*Where is it?* she wondered. *Becky's gonna hate me if I lose her camera!*

As Jess hung her backpack back up, she noticed her snacks were also missing. Her mom had given her a bag of kale chips and some trail mix for the field trip. The only things in her backpack were her lunch and the extra sweater her mom had made her bring in case it got cold.

"Come on, Jess," her mom called. "We need to rejoin the group, honey."

"But Mom—" Jess began. Then she stopped. Her mom didn't know she had Becky's camera with her. And Jess didn't want to tell her mom that she had lost it. Her mom would probably just get mad.

*What am I going to do?* Jess wondered.

# CHAPTER THREE

# CAMERA

"What do you think happened to it?" Jaylen asked.

"No clue," Jess said glumly.

"Someone could have taken it," Jaylen said.

"But who?" Jess asked. "And why would they take the trail mix and kale chips, too?"

"Yeah, what would anyone want with kale chips?" Jaylen asked. "Those things are disgusting."

*Maybe it was one of our classmates,* Jess thought. They were the only ones she knew of who could go into the student lounge.

Jess looked around. Everyone was gathering in front of a huge dinosaur skeleton. It was nearly 100 feet long from nose to tail. Its head almost touched the ceiling.

"If any of you have watched the Jurassic Park movies," their guide explained, "you'll recognize this long-necked monster. Brachiosaurus was one of the largest plant-eating dinosaurs."

As their guide talked, Jess watched her classmates closely. She hated to think one of them could have gone into her backpack and taken her sister's camera, but she had no one else to blame.

"Look," Jaylen said, nudging Jess's arm. He pointed to Aleena. "She's taking a picture."

"Come on," Jess said, pulling him toward Aleena.

But as they got closer, they could tell
Aleena was using a smartphone to take
pictures. Not a camera.

Jess and Jaylen watched their classmates
as they walked to the next exhibit. They saw
Maya pull out a camera and snap a picture.

"Did you see that?" Jess quietly
asked Jaylen.

"Yeah," Jaylen whispered. "Do you think she has your sister's camera?"

"I'm not sure," Jess whispered back. "But let's keep an eye on her."

As Maya walked to the next display of dinosaur bones, Jess and Jaylen snuck up behind her.

Maya stopped to look at an Allosaurus skull. The skull was nearly as big as she was. It had thick, pointy teeth as long as Jaylen's hands.

"Wow!" Jaylen said. "It could swallow us whole."

"Jaylen, focus," Jess said. "Or I'll really see if you'd fit in its mouth."

Jaylen gulped. Jess looked like she meant it. And Jaylen wasn't going to test whether she was serious or not. Jess was the best basketball and baseball player he knew. She could probably toss him into the Allosaurus's mouth if she wanted.

Meanwhile, Maya walked toward another exhibit. Jess and Jaylen followed.

Then Maya turned around, as if she felt someone following her. Jess and Jaylen ducked behind a couple of fake palm trees.

They watched Maya and waited for her to take another photo.

Suddenly, they both felt a hand grab their shoulders.

"Aah!" Jaylen screamed.

"Jess! Jaylen! What are you doing?" Jess's mom asked as she pulled them out from behind the trees. "You need to have more respect for the displays."

After that, Jess's mom kept a close eye on Jess and Jaylen. They didn't get a chance to

see Maya's camera up close. Not until they were back in the lounge eating lunch.

Maya was using the large screen on the back of it to flip through the photos she had taken.

Jess turned to Jaylen. "That's not Becky's camera," Jess said.

"How do you know?" Jaylen asked.

"It's too big," Jess explained. "Becky's camera is pretty small."

"But I haven't seen anyone else taking pictures," Jaylen said.

*Nuts,* Jess thought. Not only was she unable to help Becky with her extra credit but Jess had also lost her camera. Jess felt like she was turning out to be the worst sister ever.

Just then, Jaylen nudged Jess. "Look what Oscar's eating," he said.

# CHAPTER FOUR

# KALE CHIPS

Jess turned around. Sure enough, Oscar was munching on green, crunchy kale chips.

"Oscar took my camera!" Jess said, nearly shouting.

"Oscar, really?" Jaylen whispered.

"No one but my mom makes kale chips," Jess said. "They're disgusting! She always makes weird things like kale chips and seaweed smoothies. Stuff no normal person would eat. No one else would have kale chips unless they got them from my bag."

Jaylen wasn't so sure. He knew Oscar pretty well. They were in advanced math together. They were both in chess club.

And Jaylen had never known Oscar to cheat at anything. Or to steal.

But he had seen Oscar with a sandwich bag full of green chips. There was no arguing about that.

"Those look just like the chips my mom gave me," Jess insisted. "Even if he didn't take the camera, he obviously stole the chips."

Now Jess wanted to follow Oscar.

After lunch, their tour guide led them through more exhibits from the Jurassic Period. They included teeth from some of the monstrous plant eaters, such as the Apatosaurus. Its teeth were long and thin.

"They used those teeth to strip leaves off trees," Jaylen told Jess. "Kind of like rakes."

Jess looked at him and scrunched up her nose. "How do you know that?" she asked.

"Doesn't everybody?" Jaylen said.

"No, not everyone reads nerdy dinosaur books," Jess shot back.

Jaylen wasn't sure what was happening. But he could tell Jess was starting to freak out a little.

"Hey, you're not being very nice right now!" Jaylen said. "If you're just going to be snotty to me, I'm not going to help you find Becky's camera."

Jess scrunched up her nose and looked like she was about to yell at him. Then she just looked sad.

"I'm sorry. I didn't mean it," she said. "It's just that Becky's never going to like me after this."

Jaylen saw how worried his best friend was. He needed to help keep her from freaking out if they were ever going to find the camera.

"OK, OK," Jaylen said. "Don't worry about it. Let's just focus on finding the camera."

They looked around. Oscar was gone. Actually, their whole group was gone. Except for Jess's mom. She was standing

in the doorway to the next exhibit hall.
Her hands were on her hips. Her nose was
scrunched up.

"What are you two arguing about?"
she asked.

Jess and Jaylen looked at each other.
Jaylen gulped. Jess wasn't sure what would
be worse, being in trouble with Becky or with
her mom.

"Whether pterodactyls are dinosaurs or
not," Jaylen said.

"What?" Jess and her mom said at the
same time.

"That's what we were arguing about,"
Jaylen explained. "Most people think
pterodactyls are dinosaurs. But dinos didn't
fly. Pterodactyls are just huge lizards
with wings."

"Yeah, I thought they were dinos," Jess
said, playing along.

"OK," Jess's mom said slowly. "That's good to know. But you two should really keep up with the rest of the group."

Jess and Jaylen quickly caught up to their classmates.

" . . . and here we have dinosaurs from the Cretaceous Period," the tour guide was explaining. "You're probably all familiar with the Ankylosaurus, with its armored body and club-like tail.

The guide pointed toward the skeleton of a dinosaur with spikes on its tail. "But check out that Stegosaurus," he continued. "Those spikes are nearly as long as your whole arm."

As they listened, Jaylen crept toward Oscar. Jess followed him and grabbed his arm.

"What are you doing?" she whispered.

"Oscar's my friend," he whispered back, "so I'm just going to ask if he took the camera."

"But he'll lie," Jess said.

Jaylen ignored her. He wove his way through his classmates toward the front, where Oscar was standing.

"Does anyone know what those tails were used for?" the guide asked.

It was hard for Jaylen not to raise his hand. He knew the answer. But he had to focus on getting near Oscar.

Oscar raised his hand. "For defense," he said. "Their tails protected them from predators like the Tyrannosaurus rex."

"Good answer," the guide said. "Now let's go to the next room, where we have a full-scale model of a T. rex."

As everyone started moving to the next exhibit hall, Oscar turned around.

"Hey, what's up, Jaylen!" he said.

"Where did you get those green chips you were eating?" Jaylen asked.

Jess walked up behind them.

"Mrs. Reynolds gave them to me," Oscar explained. "My mom didn't pack me much for lunch, just a peanut butter sandwich."

Jess looked at Oscar suspiciously.

"Why, what's up?" Oscar asked. "They were pretty good."

"Just wondering," Jaylen said. He didn't think Oscar took the kale chips or the camera from Jess's backpack. Jess probably didn't either, but she couldn't help messing with Oscar just a little bit.

"Do you know what those chips are made of?" Jess asked.

Oscar shook his head.

"Kale," she said.

"What's that?" Oscar asked.

"Kale is the purplish-green leafy stuff that you see on your plate at fancy restaurants," Jess explained. "It's usually used as decoration."

"Ew, gross," Oscar said. "I didn't know you could eat that stuff!"

He walked away trying to wipe his tongue off with his fingers.

# BACK ON THE BUS

"Now what?" Jaylen asked Jess.

Jess wasn't sure. If someone took the camera, she was pretty sure they would be keeping it hidden. She might never find it. This day was quickly going from bad to worse.

"Becky's gonna kill me," Jess groaned.

"Come on, it's just a camera," Jaylen said.

*He doesn't get it,* Jess thought. *He has always had a brother and a sister. He doesn't have to worry whether they like him or not because they all live together. They have to like him!*

They were getting toward the end of the exhibit. The class walked past football-shaped fossilized dinosaur eggs and some T. rex teeth. Then the tour guide stopped in front of a big red question mark that was nearly as tall as the kids were.

"We really don't know why dinosaurs went extinct 65 million years ago," he explained. "But scientists have a couple of ideas . . ."

"What am I going to do?" Jess whispered to Jaylen. "The field trip is almost over, and I have no clue where Becky's camera is. She's never going to talk to me again."

As they walked back to the student lounge to pick up their backpacks, Jess looked frantic. She kept checking out each of her classmates.

"Do you think Kim took it?" she asked. "Or what about Carlos?"

Jaylen knew his friend was beyond worried. But he wasn't really sure what to do or say.

"Let's just walk around the lounge," he suggested. "Maybe it fell behind something."

As everyone else packed up, Jess and Jaylen searched the lounge. They moved chairs and looked under tables. They even started digging in the potted plants that decorated the room.

"What are you two doing now?" Jess's mom asked. "Looking for something?"

"No," Jaylen said. "Jess just—ouch!"

Jess had pinched him in the arm. "Just looking for fossils," Jess said to her mom.

Jess's mom scrunched up her nose. She didn't believe them, but she was too busy getting the rest of the kids ready to go to ask more questions.

As they walked out to their bus, Jess hung her head.

"It's gonna be all right," Jaylen said. "Remember when I broke my brother's phone?"

"Yeah," she said.

"I told the truth and everything was OK," he said.

*Well, that wasn't entirely true,* Jaylen thought. His brother Jack had gotten even with him by mixing up his entire video game collection. It took Jaylen nearly a week to get it straightened out again.

Jess wished she could believe Jaylen. But she hardly knew Becky, and Becky had trusted her. Not only would Becky hate her, but Jess was sure her dad would be pretty mad, too.

"Hey, Jess," Jaylen said, nudging her. "Look!"

Mr. Yaseen, the bus driver, was leaning against the front of the school bus. It looked like he was munching on some trail mix.

"No way!" Jess exclaimed.

Jaylen knew what Jess was thinking.

"Mr. Yaseen's been driving us to school since first grade," Jaylen said. "He wouldn't have taken Becky's camera."

But Jess wasn't listening.

"It's gotta be him!" Jess shouted.

"Jess, wait!" Jaylen called after her. But it was too late.

Jess took off. She was the first to reach the bus.

"How could you steal my sister's camera?" Jess yelled at Mr. Yaseen.

The bus driver stopped eating and stared at Jess, confused.

"That's the trail mix from my backpack," Jess continued. "You took it."

"I didn't take this from anyone's backpack," Mr. Yaseen said.

Just then, Mrs. Johnson and Jess's mom ran up to the bus.

"Jess, what's going on? What are you shouting about?" Mrs. Johnson asked.

"Mr. Yaseen has the trail mix that was missing from my bag," Jess said. She felt like she was about to cry. "He also took Becky's camera."

"What? Why do you have your stepsister's camera?" Jess's mom asked.

Mr. Yaseen reached into the bus. He pulled out a box that read "Lost & Found."

"You mean this camera?" he reached into the box and pulled out a small camera.

"That's it!" Jess said excitedly. "I thought someone took it."

Mr. Yaseen rummaged around in the box some more.

"I found a few things on the floor while you were in the museum," he explained. "This trail mix. That camera. And this key chain."

It was a green T. rex key chain that read "Fossils Rock."

"Umm," Jaylen said, grabbing the key chain, "that's mine. It must have fallen out of my backpack when it tipped over."

All of a sudden, Jess blushed. She felt embarrassed. She remembered how their backpacks had tipped over when the bus arrived at the museum.

"Oh, I'm so sorry, Mr. Yaseen," she said. "That's what must have happened to my stuff, too, I guess. I thought someone stole it."

"Then you don't mind that I was eating your trail mix?" Mr. Yaseen asked with a smile. "I was getting kind of hungry."

Jess laughed and shook her head.

Before the bus took off, Mrs. Johnson addressed her class. "First," she said, "let's thank Mrs. Reynolds for helping us out today."

Jess's mom blushed as the class said together, "Thank you, Mrs. Reynolds."

"Then, I want you to think about what you learned today," Mrs. Johnson said.

"Because for Friday, I want you to write a one-page essay about it."

Jess leaned over to Jaylen. "What are you going to write about?"

"The different dino teeth," he said. "You can tell what they chomped on by their teeth."

Jess rolled her eyes. She was tired of hearing about dinosaurs.

"What about you?" Jaylen asked.

"Not sure," Jess said. She looked worried. "I didn't take any photos for Becky's extra credit. She's still going to be mad."

"Jess, calm down," Jaylen said. "I know what it's like to have a brother and a sister. They don't stop liking you for little stuff like that."

"Are you sure?" Jess asked nervously.

"Plus, Maya was taking photos, remember?" Jaylen said. "Maybe she'll give you copies."

"Ya know, Jaylen, you were so helpful today while I was freaking out," Jess said.

"Does this mean you decided not to feed me to that Allosaurus?" Jaylen asked with a smile.

They both laughed as the bus lurched forward to take them back to school.

# NOW IT'S YOUR TURN!

1. Have you ever broken or lost something that belonged to someone else? Write a story about it. What did you lose or break? How did the person react when he or she found out what happened?

2. Imagine that you are Jaylen. What would you do to help Jess find the lost camera? Where would you look? How would you help keep her from panicking?

3. Read another Jess and Jaylen story. Pay attention to how these friends help each other out in the two stories. How are the stories similar? How are they different?

4. In this story, Jess and Jaylen use clues to try to solve a mystery. Write down all the clues they use. Are the clues helpful? Or do they point the friends in the wrong direction? Use examples from the story to explain your answer.

5. At the end of the story, Jess accuses Mr. Yaseen of stealing her sister's camera. Have you ever accused someone of doing something that they didn't do? Write a story about what happened.

6. Imagine that you are Jess. Would you tell your mom or teacher about the camera? Why or why not?

## ABOUT THE AUTHOR

Blake Hoena grew up in central Wisconsin. In his youth, he wrote stories about robots conquering the moon and trolls lumbering around the woods behind his parents' house. Later, he moved to Minnesota to pursue a master of fine arts degree in creative writing from Minnesota State University, Mankato. He now lives in Saint Paul with his wife, two kids, a dog, and a couple of cats.

Blake has written more than 60 books for children—everything from ABC books about dogs to a series of graphic novels about two alien brothers bent on conquering Earth, chapter books about Batman and Superman, and retellings of classic stories such as *Treasure Island* and *Peter Pan*.

## ABOUT THE ILLUSTRATOR

Dana Regan is originally from Lake Nebagamon, Wisconsin, and has her bachelor of fine arts degree in illustration from Washington University in Saint Louis, Missouri. She has illustrated more than 75 books and written seven early reader books, which, collectively, have sold more than 1 million copies. She lives and works in Kansas City, Missouri, with her sons, Joe and Tommy, who are a constant source of inspiration and tech support.